P9-CCZ-733

© 2003 Disney Enterprises, Inc.
All rights reserved.

Published by Scholastic Inc.
90 Old Sherman Turnpike, Danbury, Connecticut 06816.

No part of this publication may be reproduced in whole or in part, or
stored in a retrieval system, or transmitted in any form or by any means,
electronic, mechanical, photocopying, recording, or otherwise,
without written permission of the copyright holder.

SCHOLASTIC and associated designs are trademarks and/or
registered trademarks of Scholastic Inc.

For information regarding permission, write to:
Disney Licensed Publishing
114 Fifth Avenue, New York, New York 10011.

ISBN 0-7172-6801-2

Designed and produced by Bill SMITH STUDIO.

Printed in the U.S.A.
First printing, August 2003

Ready, Set, Throw!

A Story About
Being a Good Sport

by **Jacqueline A. Ball**
illustrated by
S.I. International

SCHOLASTIC INC.

New York   Toronto   London   Auckland   Sydney
Mexico City   New Delhi   Hong Kong   Buenos Aires

*B*riar Rose swept a pile of dust and crumbs out the door. "I think I'll go for a walk," she said. "It's such a calm day after that windy night."

"That sounds nice, dear," said her Aunt Flora.

"Bring back some pecans, and I'll make a pie," called her Aunt Fauna.

"Don't be too long," added her Aunt Merryweather.

"Mmm!" Briar Rose said, thinking about Merryweather's delicious pecan pies.

She soon reached a small stream. In it, she saw a snail family clinging to a leafy twig.

"The wind must have blown you into the water," Briar Rose said. "Here, let me help." She plucked the branch from the water and set it down.

"Hurry home," she told the snails. Then she giggled. "I mean, hurry as fast as snails can go."

Something furry raced by, brushing her skirt. Briar Rose looked down as two squirrels leaped across the stream.

As she watched, they scampered up a tree and disappeared down a hole. Soon the squirrels were back again.

*B*riar Rose followed the squirrels to a place where pecans lay in a thick carpet on the ground. Quickly she filled her basket. But she saw that the squirrels had to run back and forth, with nuts stuffed into their cheeks, to fill their hole.

"Oh, my," she told them. "It's going to take you all day to gather nuts. I wonder if I can help."

Briar Rose looked at the squirrels' hole. Then she picked up a nut and threw it at the hole. It landed in front of the tree.

"Hmm," she said. "I'll bet I can do better." She took aim and threw again. This time, the nut sailed right into the hole!

Surprised and pleased, she tossed another nut. It went into the hole, too. Briar Rose clapped her hands.

Then she counted out five more nuts. Two missed, but three went into the hole.

"*T*his is fun!" she exclaimed. "And the more nuts I throw, the fewer the squirrels have to carry!"

Just then her Aunt Flora came along. "You've been gone quite a while, dear."

"Sorry," said Briar Rose. "I was playing a game and lost track of time."

"What kind of game?" asked Flora.

"Try to toss pecans into that hole," Briar Rose said, pointing to the squirrel hole. "It's fun!"

$\mathcal{B}$ut Flora threw too hard, and her nuts flew past the tree. "I'm not very good at this game," she sighed.

"Don't give up, Aunt Flora," Briar Rose said. "Just do your best."

Flora took a pecan, aimed, and then threw more gently. The nut flew into the hole.

"Good for you!" exclaimed Briar Rose.

Aunt Merryweather came bustling along. "I was starting to worry," she said. "What are you two doing?"

"We're helping the squirrels," Briar Rose replied.

"And having fun," added Flora, as Briar Rose counted five nuts. "Come and play!"

"*I*f only I could use my magic," Merryweather thought.

Briar Rose's "aunts" were really fairies. They were secretly raising Briar Rose, who was actually the Princess Aurora. To keep their secret safe, they couldn't use magic.

"Here goes," Merryweather said.

"*O*h no!" she muttered. Her nut had dropped into the stream. She tried again and again but couldn't reach the hole.

"Don't give up," encouraged Briar Rose, as Flora handed Merryweather five more nuts.

Merryweather picked a pecan. She closed one eye and took careful aim. Then she threw as hard as she could. This time, the nut sailed right into the hole.

"Hooray!" cried Flora and Briar Rose.

*J*ust then Fauna strolled over to the group. "Goodness," she said. "I couldn't imagine what was keeping everyone."

"We're playing a game," explained Merryweather. "Join us."

"It's a wonderful game!" Flora said.

But Fauna said, "I'll just watch for a while."

The others went back to their game. This time, Briar Rose got all five nuts into the hole. Flora got four out of five in, and Merryweather got three out of five in.

"You're both doing so much better," Briar Rose said, complimenting them.

"This is such fun!" said Flora.

*F*auna couldn't stand it any longer. "I think I will play after all," she said.

"Wonderful!" said Briar Rose.

*F*auna threw as hard as she could. The nut zoomed over the stream. Birds dodged out of its way as it bounced off a branch, thumped against a rock, then flew—right into the squirrels' hole.

"My goodness!" exclaimed Briar Rose. The other two aunts clapped happily.

"That *was* fun!" said Fauna, jumping up and down. "I want to try again!"

"But it's my turn," Flora objected. "Oh, very well," she agreed, seeing Fauna's excitement.

*F*auna hardly heard her. She picked up her green skirt and got down on one knee. She looked right, then left. Then she rubbed a pecan between her palms.

"Fauna, just throw it," Merryweather said impatiently.

$\mathcal{A}$gain, the nut bounced, thumped, and landed in the hole. "Yes!" Fauna cried. "My trick shot worked!"

"More like a lucky shot," grumbled Flora.

Excitedly, Fauna took a nut from Flora's pile.

"That's my pile!" complained Flora. "And you're in my way."

"*O*h, sorry," said Fauna. She stepped aside and bumped into Merryweather.

"Now you spoiled *my* shot!" complained Merryweather.

"I didn't do it on purpose," Fauna protested.

"Yes, you did," Flora chimed in. "And you ruined my shot, too."

*B*riar Rose watched her aunts in dismay. They had been having so much fun, and now suddenly everyone was angry.

What would a princess do?

"We were having fun and helping the squirrels," Briar Rose reminded her aunts. "Remember? That's what's important."

"All of you tried your best, and it showed," she said. "You should all be proud of yourselves— and happy for each other."

"I'm sorry," Merryweather said. "I was jealous of you for that fancy shot, Fauna."

"I was, too," admitted Flora. "I'm sorry."

"Well, I shouldn't have bragged. And I shouldn't have been in your way," said Fauna.

*I*t was getting late. Everyone went to work, picking up the rest of the pecans. Briar Rose and her aunts filled their baskets and made sure the squirrels' hole was filled, too.

*T*hen they went back to the cottage.

Aunt Merryweather had enough pecans to bake two pies. Soon everyone was full of pie and piping hot tea.

"How *did* you do that shot, Fauna?" Flora wanted to know.

"It's easy," Fauna said, jumping up. "I'll show you." She grabbed an egg and started to wind up.

"No!" everyone shouted at the same time, ducking for cover.

"Let's save it for another game," said Briar Rose with a smile.

The End